S0-BSE-870

DISCARDED

Watch Me Go!

MY SCOOTER

Victor Blaine

PowerKiDS press.

New York

Public Library
Incorporated 1862
Barrie, Ontario

Published in 2015 by The Rosen Publishing Group, Inc.
29 East 21st Street, New York, NY 10010

Copyright © 2015 by The Rosen Publishing Group, Inc.

All rights reserved. No part of this book may be reproduced in any form without permission in writing from the publisher, except by a reviewer.

First Edition

Editor: Sarah Machajewski
Book Design: Mickey Harmon

Photo Credits: Cover, pp. 1, 21 Stephen Simpson/Taxi/Getty Images; p. 5 jambro/Shutterstock.com; p. 6 Frank Siteman/age fotostock/Getty Images; p. 9 © iStockphoto.com/donkeyru; p. 10 Szasz-Fabian Jozsef/Shutterstock.com; p. 13 Studio 37/Shutterstock.com; p. 14 © iStockphoto.com/jessicaphoto; pp. 17, 18 Stephen Simpson/Iconica/Getty Images; p. 22 Pavel L Photo and Video/Shutterstock.com.

Library of Congress Cataloging-in-Publication Data

Blaine, Victor.
My scooter / by Victor Blaine.
p. cm. — (Watch me go!)
Includes index.
ISBN 978-1-4994-0260-5 (pbk.)
ISBN 978-1-4994-0240-7 (6-pack)
ISBN 978-1-4994-0253-7 (library binding)
1. Scootering — Juvenile literature. 2. Scooters — Juvenile literature. I. Title.
GV859.77 B53 2015
796.6—d23

Manufactured in the United States of America

CPSIA Compliance Information: Batch #CW15PK: For Further Information contact Rosen Publishing, New York, New York at 1-800-237-9932

CONTENTS

Do you have a scooter?
A scooter is a fun way
to get from place to place.

You can ride one by yourself.
You can also ride one
with your friends.

Most scooters are called kick scooters. You move them with your feet.

Scooter riders stand on the **deck**. The deck is long and flat.

Scooter wheels are near your feet.

Some scooters have two wheels. Other scooters have three or four wheels!

Scooters can move fast. Riders slow down by using the brake.

brake

Some riders like to do tricks. Jumping with the whole scooter is called a bunny hop.

A **manual** is a trick where a rider uses only the back wheel.

Riding a scooter is a lot of fun. Remember to wear a helmet!

WORDS TO KNOW

deck

manual

INDEX

WEBSITES

Due to the changing nature of Internet links, PowerKids Press has developed an online list of websites related to the subject of this book. This site is updated regularly. Please use this link to access the list: www.powerkidslinks.com/wmg/scoo